MW00991428

Hoot and Peep

Lita Judge

Dial Books for Young Readers

Peep was finally old enough to join her big brother, Hoot, on the rooftops.

It's the perfect night to teach Peeps all my owly wisdom, thought Hoot.

Peep thought it was the perfect night to sing about the magic of the moonbeams.

"Schweep," she peeped.

"No, no, no! It goes like this, Peeps. First, we are owls. We say Hooo.

"Second, we ALWAYS say Hooo.

"Lastly, we ONLY say Hooo."

There! He was done imparting all his owly wisdom.

"Listen to me, Peeps.
I'm older. I know more.
We owls simply say Hooo."

"Hooo! Hooo! Hooooo!

Hooo means hello,
good-bye, good
morning, and good night.
Hooo is the only way to
say EVERYTHING!"

Hoot forgot,
owls never shout.
Peep had nothing
to say and just
flew away.

The problem with Peep, thought Hoot, is she won't listen to my owly wisdom.

The problem with Hoot,
thought Peep, is he doesn't
believe in singing about
the mystery of things.

Peep believed in
whispering to an
ancient wind,
"Schweeep dingity
dong, schweeep
dingity dong."

And singing with the slip-slap of waves against stone. "Slippity slap, slippity slap."

Hoot knew he was right, that is, until he started missing Peep's songs.

Without Peep to listen, there didn't seem to be a point in saying Hooo anymore.

dingity-dong

Then Hoot heard Peep's sweet voice drifting on the wind. The sound was like magic.

"Schweepity ding,

schweepity dong."

Hoot realized he had
made a big mistake!
Little sisters have their
own owly wisdom.

"Can you teach
me your song,
Peeps?"

"Slippity slap."

Soon the night wind rang
with songs of joy and love
and magic things.

Hoot and Peep sang together,
but each in their very own
owly way.

And that, they thought,
was why it was a
perfect night.

For Dave

DIAL BOOKS FOR YOUNG READERS
Penguin Young Readers Group
An imprint of Penguin Random House, LLC
375 Hudson Street | New York, New York 10014

Text and pictures copyright © 2016 by Lita Judge

Library of Congress Cataloging-in-Publication Data
Judge, Lita, author, illustrator.   Hoot and Peep / by Lita Judge.   pages cm
Summary: "Hoot the owl is excited to teach his younger sister all of his wisdom—but much to his annoyance, Peep is more interested in capturing the magic of the world around her than in listening to his advice"— Provided by publisher.
ISBN 978-0-525-42837-4 (hardcover)
[1. Owls—Fiction. 2. Brothers and sisters—Fiction. 3. Individuality—Fiction.] I. Title.
PZ7.J894Hoo 2016   [E]—dc23   2015000612

Manufactured in China on acid-free paper
3   4   5   6   7   8   9   10

Design by Jennifer Kelly
Text set in Berling LT Std

The illustrations were created using watercolors with a few digital finishing touches.

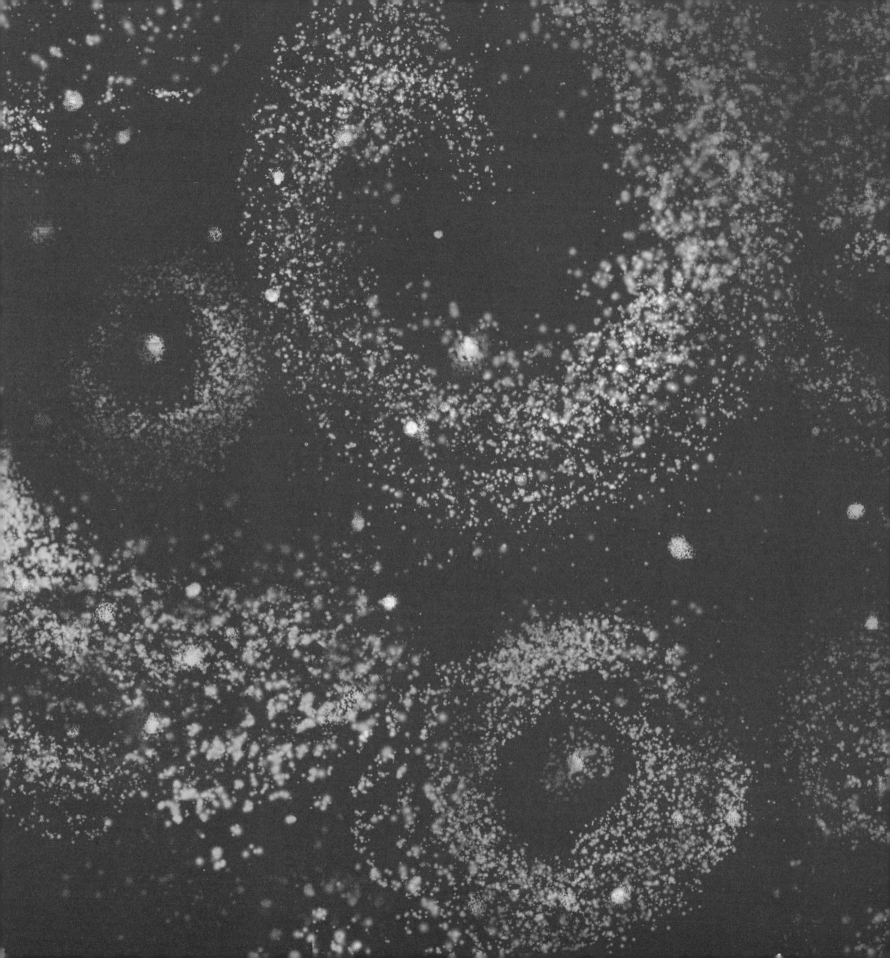